# A GATOR took my TOOTHBRUSH

Sweetwater Books · An imprint of Cedar Fort, Inc. · Springville, Utah

A little boy sat on the edge
of his bed, playing with his toys.

When his mom walked in, he wasn't
surprised that she made a gasping noise.

"A gator took my toothbrush!
There was nothing I could do.

He has so many pointy teeth, I
had to wait till he was through."

"A beaver was in my bathtub. I'd
have joined him if I could,

but there wasn't room for both of
us. He'd filled it up with wood!"

"A tarantula used my towel,
but he didn't think to ask.

I bet to dry his eight hairy
legs is not an easy task."

"A lion had my hairbrush.
I bet it is a pain

to roar and prowl and rule the
pride with such a matted mane."

"A panda put on my pj's, but
they didn't fit quite right.

She took my favorite blue ones since
she's tired of black and white."

"A porcupine poached my pillow.
Of that you can be sure.

What other reason could there be
for all the feathers on the floor?"

"A bat flew off with my night light,
which doesn't come as a surprise.

She likes it better in the dark.
I bet it hurts her eyes."

"What a wonderful imagination!"
his mom said with a smile,

"But the only creature in your
room is your toy crocodile."

"Tomorrow is the first day of
school, and it's starting to get late.

It's important to get lots of sleep
so you can concentrate."

"But just in case, I'll go downstairs and make a phone call to the zoo.

Once you've bathed and brushed your teeth, I'll come to check on you."

When she closed the
door behind her, the boy said,
"The coast is clear!"

Then one by one the
animals slowly started to appear.

"That really was a close one.
Panda, please go get a broom.

I'll let you all sleep here tonight
if you help me clean my room."

For my beautiful wife, Emily, and for
Brayden and Adaline, my wonderful children
who inspire and amaze me every day.

–Brandon

Text © 2020 Brandon Frisby
Illustrations © 2020 Wes Wheeler
All rights reserved.

The opinions and views expressed herein belong solely to the author and do not necessarily represent the opinions or views of Cedar Fort, Inc. Permission for the use of sources, graphics, and photos is also solely the responsibility of the author.

ISBN 13: 978-1-4621-3697-1

Published by Sweetwater Books, an imprint of Cedar Fort, Inc.
2373 W. 700 S., Springville, UT 84663
Distributed by Cedar Fort, Inc., www.cedarfort.com

Library of Congress Control Number: 2020941183

Cover design and typesetting by Wes Wheeler
Cover design © 2020 Cedar Fort, Inc.

Printed in the United States of America

10 9 8 7 6 5 4 3 2 1

Printed on acid-free paper